W9-AWH-680

DATE DUE

E
Mon   Moncure, Jane Belk
       My "b" sound box

ENCYCLOPAEDIA BRITANNICA
EDUCATIONAL CORPORATION
310 S. Michigan Avenue • Chicago, Illinois 60604

85351

My **b** Sound Box

by Jane Belk Moncure
illustrated by Linda Sommers

THE CHILD'S WORLD

MANKATO, MN 56001

Library of Congress Cataloging in Publication Data

Moncure, Jane Belk.
My b sound box.

(Sound box books)
SUMMARY: A little girl fills her sound box with many words beginning with the letter "b".
[1. Alphabet books] I. Sommers, Linda.
II. Title. III. Series.
PZ7.M739Myb   [E]   77-23588
ISBN 0-913778-92-3 -1991 Edition

My "b" Sound Box

(Blends are included in this book.)

Little  had a box.

"I will find things that begin with my "b" sound," she said.

"I will put them into

my sound  box."

Little b put on her bonnet

and went for a walk.

Little found a bird

and a

birdbath.

Did she put the bird and the birdbath

into the box?

She did!

Little found a bunny.

Did she put the bunny into the box with the
bird and
the birdbath?

She did!

Then Little **b** heard a sound, "Bzzzz."

It was a bee.

She put the bee into the box - - -

carefully!

Next, she found a baby baboon in a tree.

The baby baboon was eating a  banana.

"I will put you into my box," said Little b.

The box was so big she could hardly carry it.

She found a  bicycle

with a 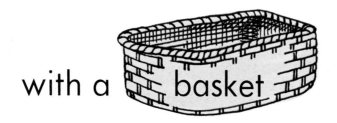 basket

on the back.

She put the  box

into the basket

and rode the bicycle

over a big bump!

The baby baboon,

the bunny,

and the bird

bounced out of the box

And Little b bounced off the bicycle.

"That was a bad bump," she said.

Then she saw a 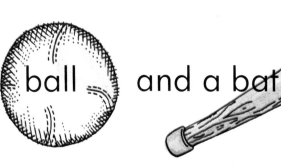 ball and a bat.

"Let's play ball!" she said.

And they did.

The baby baboon hit the ball with the bat.

It bounced into a bush.

Something was behind the bush.

It was a  bear.

Bear gave the ball to Little b.

"Thank you, Bear," she said.

She put the bear, the bush, and the ball into the box.
She put the baby baboon, the bat, the bird, the
birdbath, and the bunny back, too.

The bee said,
"Buzz, buzz,
this box
may break."

"I must find something bigger," said Little

24

She rode her bicycle over the

bridge

box

Under the bridge, she saw a boat, a big, big boat.
She jumped into the boat and took the things out
of her box. "This is big enough," she said,
"big enough for all of us."

And it was!

Can you read these words with Little ?

balloon

barn

butterfly

bathtub

bell

bug

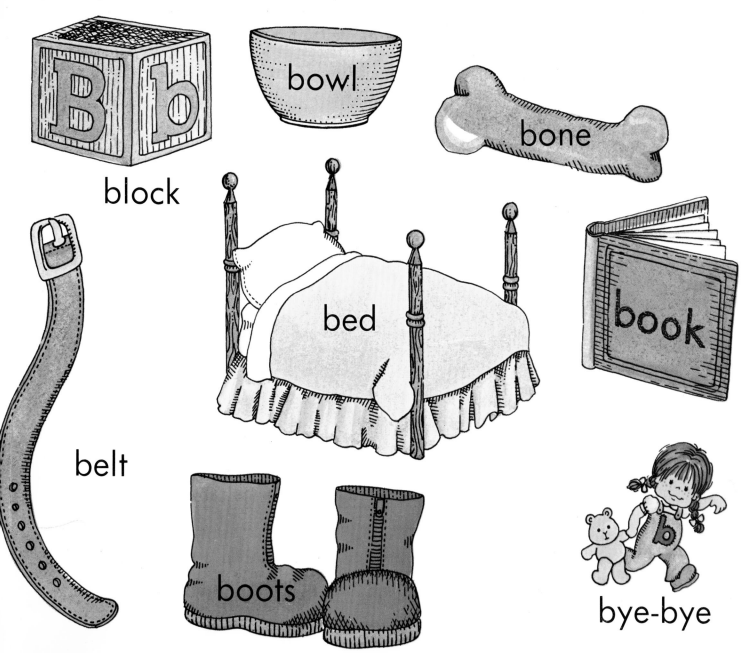

block

bowl

bone

belt

bed

book

boots

bye-bye

29

About the Author

Jane Belk Moncure, author of many books and stories for young children, is a graduate of Virginia Commonwealth University and Columbia University. She has taught nursery, kindergarten and primary children in Europe and America. Mrs. Moncure has taught early childhood education while serving on the faculties of Virginia Commonwealth University and the University of Richmond. She was the first president of the Virginia Association for Early Childhood Education and has been recognized widely for her services to young children. She is married to Dr. James A. Moncure, Vice President of Elon College, and currently teaches in Burlington, North Carolina.